THE Invisible MISTAKECASE

by CHARISE MERICLE HARPER

Houghton Mifflin Company
Boston 2005

FOR TARYN,
Whose 5,000 loving kisses for Baby Luther
helped me finish this book

Copyright © 2005 by Charise Mericle Harper

All rights reserved. For information about permission to reproduce selections from this book, write to
Permissions, Houghton Mifflin Company, 215 Park Avenue South, New York, New York 10003.

www.houghtonmifflinbooks.com

The illustrations are acrylic and collage.

Library of Congress Cataloging-in-Publication Data
Harper, Charise Mericle.
The invisible mistakecase / written and illustrated by Charise Mericle Harper.
p. cm.
Summary: After calling her friend "big pink baby," Charlotte, a young alligator, feels terrible until
Grandpa tells her about a useful way to learn from her mistakes.
ISBN-10: 0-618-44885-3
[1. Alligators—Fiction. 2. Conduct of life—Fiction. 3. Grandfathers—Fiction.] I. Title.
PZ7.H231323In 2005   [Fic]—dc22   2004025122

ISBN-13: 978-0618-44885-2

Printed in Singapore
TWP 10 9 8 7 6 5 4 3 2 1

TODAY WAS A BEAUTIFUL DAY.

The sun was shining, the birds were tweeting, and the clouds in the sky were puffy and white.

But even on beautiful days, bad things can happen. And a bad thing did happen right on the front steps of 24 West Vine Street. An alligator named Charlotte called her best friend, Kate, a big pink baby. And then right after she said it, Charlotte stomped into her house and slammed the front door!

"I won't cry," said Kate,
but of course she cried all
the way home.

OH DEAR!

Seven seconds after she slammed the door, Charlotte felt a little bad.

And eight, nine, ten seconds later she felt even worse. She wished she hadn't called her best friend, Kate, a big pink baby. In fact, she wished it so hard, it pushed all the other wishes she had right out of her head.

Sometimes a big wish can move down a throat and into a stomach.
Charlotte was so filled up with her wish that she couldn't even
eat her dinner, which was pizza and French fries.

GRANDPA

Charlotte lived with her grandpa. Grandpa was a smart man. He knew a little about a lot of things and a lot about a little alligator named Charlotte.

What Grandpa Knows

WHAT CHARLOTTE LOVES TO DO

READ

CHARLOTTE'S FAVORITE GAME — SKIPPING

FOODS THAT CHARLOTTE LIKES

CHARLOTTE'S FAVORITE SONGS — LA, LA, LA

CHARLOTTE'S BEST FRIEND

FOOD CHARLOTTE DOESN'T LIKE — PEAS

THINGS THAT SCARE CHARLOTTE

CHARLOTTE'S FAVORITE COLOR

EVERYTHING ELSE

Grandpa could tell something was wrong. He made Charlotte sit down and tell him all about it. "Oh, Grandpa!" cried Charlotte, and she told him the whole story, in between sniffles and snorts. "Ah," said Grandpa, "this is one for the invisible mistakecase." "The what?" sobbed Charlotte. "I will tell you," said Grandpa, and then he did because he always kept his word.

"The invisible mistakecase is a suitcase where I keep all the mistakes I've made once and never want to make again. I carry it everywhere I go. It's right here," said Grandpa, and he pointed to an empty space on the floor. Charlotte squinted her eyes but couldn't see anything. "What's in it?" she asked.

"Well, let's see," said Grandpa, and he opened his invisible mistakecase—at least it looked like he did.

"I'll just pick out one thing to show you and then it's time for dessert."

Grandpa was very fond of dessert.

COMPLETELY EMPTY

"Ah, here's my piece of pie," said Grandpa, holding up something invisible. Then he shut the suitcase up tight so Charlotte couldn't see inside—which she couldn't anyway because it was invisible. And with Charlotte right there on his knee he told her a story about pie:

When I was a young alligator (Grandpa said), my mama made a pie for dessert every Sunday night. The pie was just the right size for everyone to have one piece on Sunday and then have the leftovers for dessert on Monday. I liked all kinds of pies, but my favorite was cherry pie.

One Sunday night, after a particularly delicious cherry pie dessert,
I couldn't sleep. I kept thinking about the pie downstairs and how
I'd like to have just one more tasty bite.

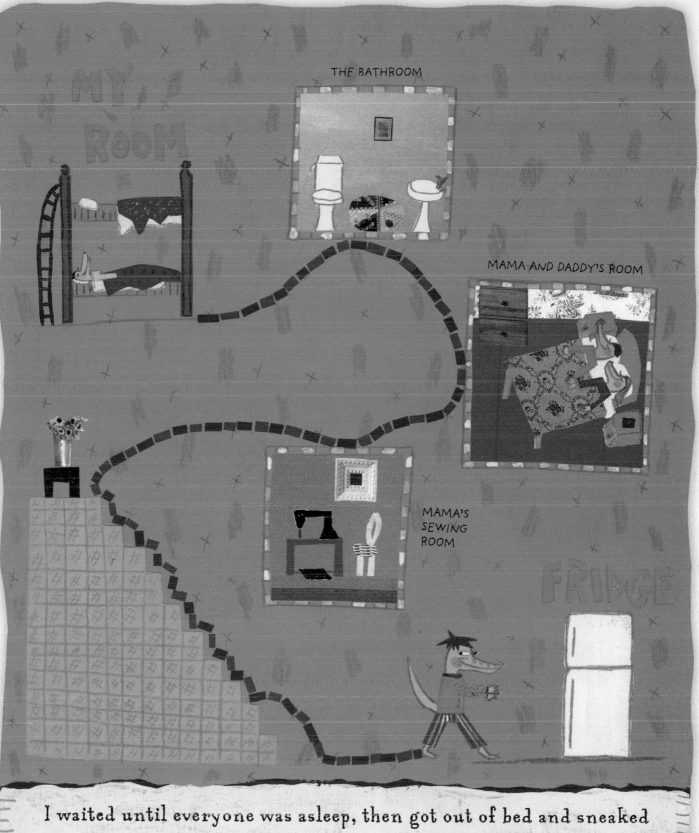

I waited until everyone was asleep, then got out of bed and sneaked down to the refrigerator.

There was the pie. I cut a little piece off the edge. It was yummy! But
then the pie looked crooked. I had to cut and eat three more pieces

until it looked straight again. I was sure no one would notice and I
went to back to bed with a warm, happy tummy.

On Monday night Mama brought out the leftover cherry pie. It looked very small. "Who ate the pie?" she asked. Everyone, including me said, "Not me." Of course I was lying. That night we all had teeny tiny pieces of pie and I went to bed with a funny feeling in my tummy.

Every day for five days Mama asked me and my brother, John, the
same question: "Did you eat the pie?" "It wasn't me," I answered,
and then I looked at John suspiciously so Mama would maybe think
it was him that ate the pie. "I didn't eat it," said John. "Maybe it
was a ghost."

And every night I went to bed with a tummy-ache and had bad dreams.

Finally on the sixth day when Mama asked, "Did you eat the pie?" I said, "Yes, it was me." Mama was surprised. "I thought it was John," she said. John said, "I knew it wasn't me."

I wasn't allowed to have dessert for a whole week, but you know what? My tummy-aches and bad dreams stopped right away. I decided that even though I could lie better than John could tell the truth, I would try to never lie again.

And just so I'll never forget that promise, I keep this piece of pie in my suitcase. Anytime I worry I might tell even a teeny tiny lie, I open up my suitcase, see this piece of pie, and remember my promise.

"I'll never lie because of this pie," said Grandpa, and then
he put his invisible pie back into his invisible mistakecase.

"How about some dessert?" he asked. Charlotte was suddenly feeling a little bit hungry.

After a delicious ice cream dessert

and a warm soapy bubble bath, it was time for bed.

"Is it heavy?" asked Charlotte, pointing down to the empty space beside Grandpa. "Not at all." Grandpa smiled. "In fact, I'll tell you a secret," he said, and with Grandpa whispering secrets about heavy on the inside and light on the outside, Charlotte fell fast asleep.

THE NEXT DAY WAS GLOOMY.

The wind was blowing, the rain was falling, and the clouds were like a big, gray pancake covering the whole sky.

But even on gloomy days,
good things can happen.

COMPLETELY
EMPTY

Charlotte skipped with happy steps
all the way to her best friend Kate's house.
Every couple of minutes she smiled, looked down,
and swung her arm like she was holding a suitcase,
but she wasn't—her hand was completely empty.

When she got to Kate's house, she took a deep breath, climbed
the stairs, and knocked on the door. Kate opened the door
just a crack. She didn't want Charlotte to call her a big pink baby
all over again.

But Charlotte didn't. "I'm so sorry for calling you a big pink baby,"
said Charlotte. "I promise never to call you a name again! And just
so I don't forget I made up this rhyme:

I'll call Kate, KATE in sun,
I'll call Kate, KATE in rain,
I'll forever call Kate, KATE,
    AND NOT A NAME AGAIN

and I put it on a nametag right here inside my invisible
mistakecase." "Really?" said Kate, and she squinted her eyes to
where Charlotte was pointing. "It's a suitcase," said Charlotte,
"but it's not at all heavy."

GOOD.

FRIENDS FOREVER

And then she told Kate
all about it, right after she
walked in the front door.